RO1055 67359

THE UGLY TRUCKLING

Written and Illustrated by

DAVID GORDON

LAURA GERINGER BOOKS

An Imprint of HarperCollinsPublishers

Manufactured in China by South China Printing Company Ltd.
All rights reserved.   www.harperchildrens.com
Library of Congress Cataloging-in-Publication Data   Gordon, David, date.
The ugly truckling / written and illustrated by David Gordon.—1st ed.   p.   cm.
Summary: Teased by her brothers and sisters for being so different, an ugly truckling fears that
she will never be a good truck, and sets out into the world to discover what she might be.
ISBN 0-06-054600-X — ISBN 0-06-054601-8 (lib. bdg.)
[1. Trucks—Fiction. 2. Airplanes—Fiction. 3. Self-esteem—Fiction. 4. Brothers and sisters—
Fiction.] I. Title. PZ7.G6547Ug 2004 [E]—dc21 2003006804 CIP AC
Typography by Alicia Mikles 1 2 3 4 5 6 7 8 9 10 ❖ First Edition

For Marcia

Special thanks for all your love and support:

Susan, Dad and Marcia Gordon, Jamie and Tony, Joey-boy, Josh and Eve,

Hava and Jason, Lethi and Eric, Rebecca and Michael, Carrie and Portia and Tatiana, Laurie Mcfarlen,

Bob and Jay, Steve Wunsh and Steve Gordon, Pete de Seve, Dice and Vince.

Way out west,
where the vehicles roam
from ranch to ranch,

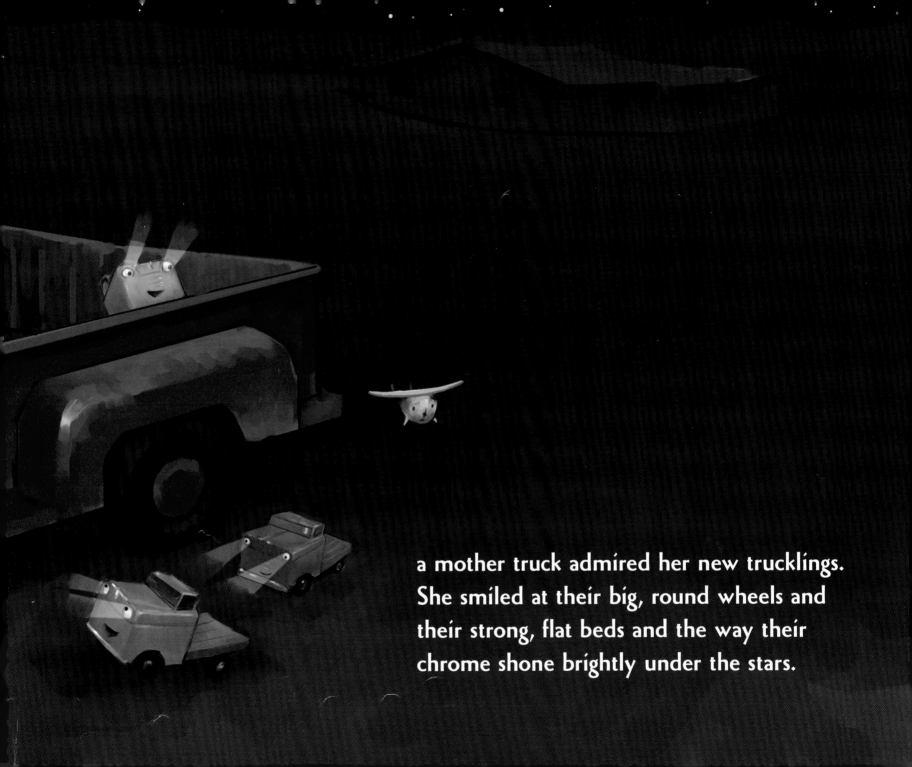

a mother truck admired her new trucklings. She smiled at their big, round wheels and their strong, flat beds and the way their chrome shone brightly under the stars.

But one of the trucklings was not like her brothers and sisters. This truckling's wheels were small and narrow. She didn't have a strong, flat bed. And her chrome did not shine brightly under the stars.

To make matters worse, two strange beams stuck out from the sides of her body. She was an ugly truckling.

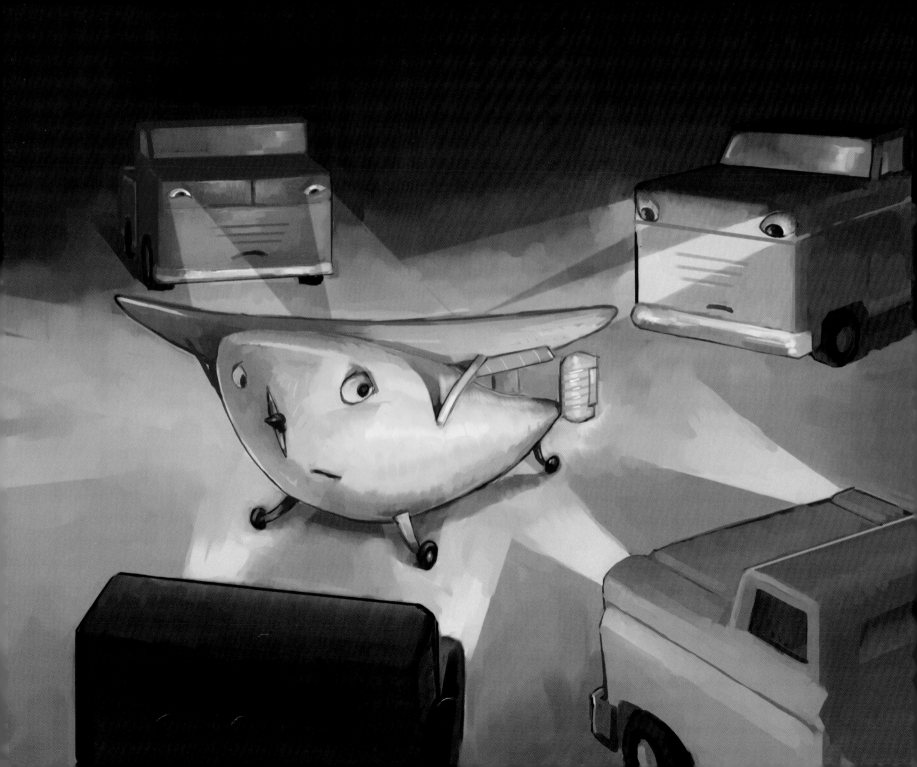

The next morning the little trucklings
followed their mother, carrying rocks and bricks
and wood in their little truck beds.

But the ugly truckling could barely haul a small bale of hay or pull a log. All the other little trucklings laughed at her.

"Why do you have three wheels instead of four?" asked one of her brothers.

"And why do you carry hay on your head?" asked her sister.
"You'll never be a good truck," said another brother.
The ugly truckling was very sad. She was afraid he was right.

So late one night, when the sky was black and starless,
the ugly truckling sped away.

The next morning she met a tractor.

"Good morning," said the ugly truckling.
"Who are you?"

"I'm a tractor," said the tractor.

"Am I a tractor too?"

"You're no tractor. Tractors don't
have propellers on their noses."

"Oh," sighed the ugly truckling.
And she sped away.

Then the ugly truckling met a cow.
"Good afternoon," said the ugly truckling. "Who are you?"
"I'm a cow," said the cow.

"Am I a cow too?"

"You're no cow. Cows have legs, not wheels."

"Oh," said the ugly truckling. And she sped away, a little slower than before.

The ugly truckling drove for hours until she reached a pond. There she met a windmill.

"Good evening," said the ugly truckling sadly. "Who are you?"

"I'm a windmill," said the windmill.

"Am I a windmill too?"

"You're no windmill. Windmills are tall and have big spokes."

"Oh," said the ugly truckling. And she slowly started to roll away.

"Wait," said the windmill. "Why are you so sad?"
"I'm not a tractor. I'm not a cow. I'm not a windmill. And
I don't think I'm a truck either. I don't know who I am."

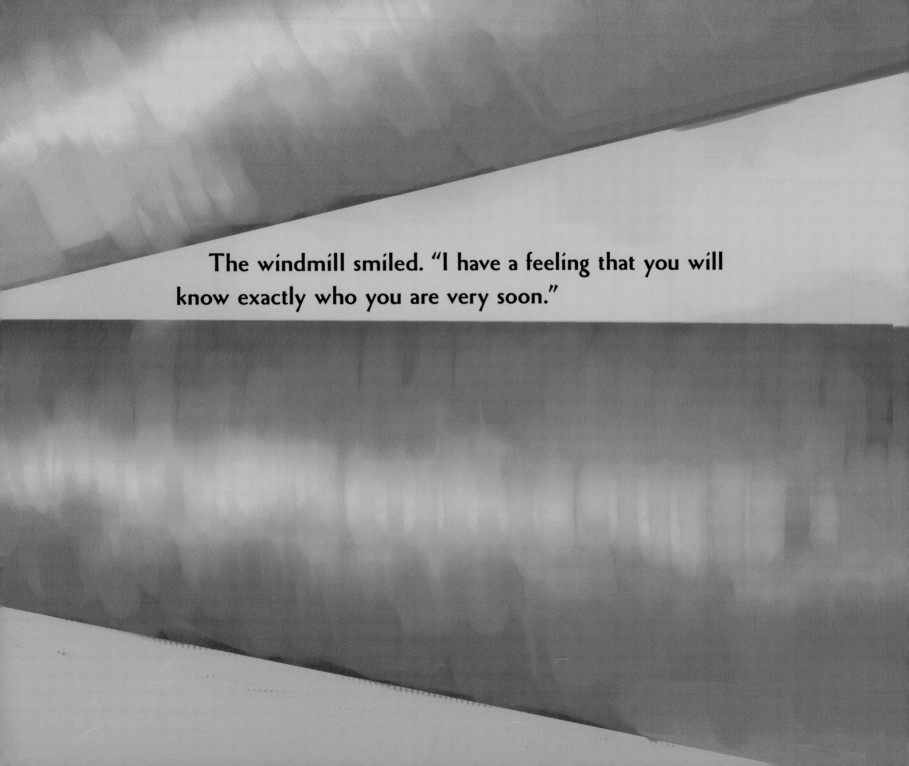

The windmill smiled. "I have a feeling that you will know exactly who you are very soon."

The ugly truckling looked at her reflection in the pond.
Suddenly she heard a loud roar overhead and looked up.

The windmill was right. She wasn't an ugly truckling after all. She was a beautiful airplane.

And so she flew away with the other airplanes . . .

into a sky full of stars.